ADVENTURE HUNTERS

Tales Of Daring-Do

Edited By Briony Kearney

First published in Great Britain in 2022 by:

Young Writers
Remus House
Coltsfoot Drive
Peterborough
PE2 9BF
Telephone: 01733 890066
Website: www.youngwriters.co.uk

All Rights Reserved
Book Design by Ashley Janson
© Copyright Contributors 2022
Softback ISBN 978-1-80015-888-7

Printed and bound in the UK by BookPrintingUK
Website: www.bookprintinguk.com
YB0500E

FOREWORD

Are you searching for adventure? Then come right this way – fun and daring deeds await! It's very simple, all you have to do is turn the page and you'll be transported into a wealth of amazing adventure stories.

Is it magic? Is it a trick? No! It's all down to the skill and imagination of primary school pupils from around the country. For our latest competition Adventure Hunters, we gave them the task of writing a story on any topic, and to do it in just 100 words! I think you'll agree they've achieved that brilliantly – this book is jam-packed with exciting and thrilling tales.

These young authors have brought their ideas to life using only their words. This is the power of creativity and it gives us life too! Here at Young Writers we want to pass our love of the written word onto the next generation and what better way to do that than to celebrate their writing by publishing it in a book!

It sets their work free from homework books and notepads and puts it where it deserves to be – out in the world and preserved forever! Each awesome author in this book should be super proud of themselves, and now they've got proof of their ideas and their creativity in black and white, to look back on in years to come!

We hope you enjoy this book as much as we have! Now it's time to let imagination take control, so read on...

CONTENTS

Holtsmere End Junior School, Woodhall Farm

Daisy Groom (9)	57
Grace Groom (7)	58
Amy Diggines (11)	59
Andreea Abunei (9)	60
Antonina Grygiel (9)	61
Oliver Potter (9)	62
Stella French (9)	63
Abby Thapa (8)	64
Melissa Stefanoaia (9)	65
Skye Kennie (11)	66
Uthman Fatih (10)	67
Aanya Chandarana (8)	68
Ryan Gay (9)	69
James Hart (11)	70
Lily-Alice Stiff (9)	71
Millie Beamon (11)	72
Charlotte Mitchell (9)	73
T'iarah Bowen (8)	74
Nelly Wheller (10)	75
Logan Wallace (8)	76
Iraklis Karamitsos (8)	77
Sara Stevlik (7)	78

New Monkland Primary School, Glenmavis

Charlotte Bianchi (11)	79
Mollie Chaddock (10)	80
Freya Blair (11)	81
Sufyaan Sharif (11)	82
Lola Hunt (11)	83
Ellie McFarland (10)	84
Rudy Wood (11)	85
Mitchell Scott Manson (11)	86
Kara Beggs (11)	87
Holly McDougall (11)	88
Olivia Brownlie (11)	89
Evan McAuley (11)	90
Lauren McKennan (10)	91
Evie Hutton (11)	92
Skye Young (11)	93

Pheasey Park Farm Primary School, Great Barr

Niamh Murphy (8)	94
Leah Wacogne (8)	95
Grayson Franklin (8)	96
Henry Newey (8)	97
Maicie Lees (9)	98
Lola-rose Wheeldon	99
Solomon Georgiou (9)	100
Abigail Baingana (8)	101
Theo Dwyer (8)	102
Grace Hart (8)	103
Paige Webb (9)	104
Ruby Walsh (8)	105
Esme Tallulah Bagnall (8)	106
Kimiya Knight	107
Alfie Silver (8)	108
Skyla'Jai Nevers-Hamilton (9)	109
Brendan Swain (8)	110
Scarlett Owen (8)	111
Joshua Goulbourne (9)	112
Evie Lester (9)	113
Scarlett Carpenter (8)	114
Harshiv Tuteja (8)	115
Muhammad Ayaan Arshad (9)	116
Michael Dawes (9)	117
Ryley Bates (8)	118
Ameya Lamichhane (9)	119
Mariam Georgiou (8)	120
Gracie Doidge (8)	121
Ruby Hill (9)	122
Imogen Tang	123
Lewis Wilkins	124
Owen Howard (9)	125
Francesca Hall (8)	126
Amy Mather	127
Dylan Minshull	128
Felicity Mckeon (8)	129
Lexi Ashford (8)	130
Lilly William (8)	131
Abby Skelton	132
Ethan Allmark (9)	133
Harrison Oneill	134

Red House School, Norton

Ethan Reddivari (10)	135
William Moore (7)	136
Leon Tanttari (8)	137
Genevieve Reily (10)	138
Hugo Duncan-Whitfield (11)	139
Naina Kurup (10)	140
Maia Olbrich (10)	141
Eddison Williams (10)	142
Adam Khaliq (10)	143
Harry Oo (10)	144
Isobel Haywood (10)	145
Finley Williamson (11)	146
Luke Gardner (11)	147
Iris McGlynn (10)	148
Erin Hodgson (10)	149
Isabella Riley (10)	150
Kayden Duffey (10)	151
Faith Hall (11)	152
Jenson Harte (10)	153
Brontë Marin (10)	154
Dylan Hodgson Wood (10)	155
Robynne Mclaren (11)	156
Samira Arun (8)	157
Ashton Chapman (9)	158
Philippa Vaux (10)	159
Tobias MacDonald (10)	160
William Robinson (9)	161
Harry Bobby Winspear (10)	162
Jessica Howlett (9)	163

St John's Primary School, Liverpool

Kashaya Yakou (11)	164
Dana Conroy (10)	165
Maya Cyron (10)	166
Patrick O'Sullivan (11)	167
Antoni Warcholik (10)	168
Laurie Faragher (10)	169
Lola Jarman (11)	170
Jacob Draper (11)	171
Hawi Haydar (10)	172

John Shaw (10)	173
Tomas Lee (10)	174
Sammy Draper (10)	175

The Promised Neverland

Running through the orphanage, looking for an escape to get away from her. Our orphanage mother. Searching through every hallway, going through every door and not finding an exit. There she was, she'd found us.

Running, running away. "She found us, she's got us," I whispered. Our orphanage mother got closer and closer but still... still we had time to escape! Although she was still coming to get us.

My friend Norman yelled to our orphanage mother, "You can't keep us here forever to be eaten! We will find an escape!" he yelled. It echoed through the hallway.

Isabella Kavak (11)

Anagh Coar Primary School, Anagh Coar

Find The Truth

It was an icy cold Thursday morning when Lainie decided to start her extraordinary, ambitious quest to see if she may be the lost princess. She packed all the essentials, said goodbye to her beloved mother, and walked out of the door. A couple of hours later, Lainie reached her destination.
She took in the view; it was blazing hot and had cactuses everywhere. Lainie started walking toward the castle that, by now, she could see - but, suddenly, she got spiked by a cactus. Lainie kept walking, trying to get to the castle before sunset. But she never got there...

Lainie Savage (10)
Anagh Coar Primary School, Anagh Coar

The Missing Compass

I heard a deafening roar. Yesterday, 4:50 on the dot, something extraordinary happened. I was told about a compass, it had to do with my family - me and my old dad, Daniel. It belonged to my grandpa. Three hours later, I was home alone so decided to head to the jungle where the compass was located.

It took me a while to find where I was going. Eventually, I found the hole where the compass lay. Suddenly, a large carnivore appeared in the distance. As I hid behind a tree, it strolled along. I grasped the compass and sprinted home.

Madyson Halsall (10)
Anagh Coar Primary School, Anagh Coar

Lost Dog

Feeling devastated, Lisa was sick of waiting. She had to go out and find her dog, Charlie. He'd been missing for a month and her fear was growing larger. Last she saw him was before someone broke in... She grabbed her coat and sped out. She struggled to run through the forest. Noises spun around the trees. Not long after, she met a gloomy, deserted building. Graffiti covered almost the whole dull building. There was no other way to get past, so she had to enter. Inside there was only one candle - and someone blew it out.

Katya Pais (10)
Anagh Coar Primary School, Anagh Coar

COVID Hero

The year the world changed forever: 2019. Two years later, someone dropped from the sky. You could see a shape in the distance. People around were curious. The hero in the distance had a box that glowed so bright. He took out the magic stick and started to wave it around, and the gloomy sky turned bright. The hero's magic stick started to break the curse: no more COVID. He was a hero who saved the world and the world was bright once again. So many people were happy to hug again and all children could go back to school.

Rebecca Foster (10)
Anagh Coar Primary School, Anagh Coar

Little Lost Forest

Once there were two little girls lost in the forest. They were called Millie and Lilly. Millie was a shy girl and Lilly was a bit older and wiser than Millie. So, one day, when playing in the forest, Millie and Lilly were just normal children having fun when they got a bit curious. They'd forgotten which way they came into the forest. They weren't prepared, for the trees looked all the same. So, soon, they became deserted and scared of their location. But Millie remembered she had a phone on her and felt better!

Mia Shimmin (8)
Anagh Coar Primary School, Anagh Coar

Eddie The Elf

Once, there was a girl called Eddie. Eddie loved Christmas! She had always wanted to meet Santa. One Christmas, Eddie decided to see if she could see the real Santa. At night, she tiptoed down the steps... and heard something coming down the chimney! It was Santa!

"Eddie, why are you up so late?"

"Um, I just wanted to... um..."

Santa took out a funny device and it pointed to Eddie. "Oh wow, your Christmas spirit is high!"

"Well, I do like Christmas a lot."

"Now get back to bed!"

"Okay, Nick." And that is how Eddie became an elf!

Emili Kristopaitis (8)
Barnes Junior School, Sunderland

Secret Treasure Hunt

Once upon a time, there was a girl called Starlight. She was like, "It's just an extraordinary day. There's, like, nothing to do."
She was at home and then something caught her eye. It was coming from the downstairs cell. So she went downstairs to the cell and opened the door and it was a map. It said on the paper: *Abracadabra*. When Starlight said that, it took her to a gloomy forest. Straight, left, twirl, right, and *X* marks the spot. She dug up the treasure and it was a magic mixer! She made some potions. What an adventure!

Umaymah Zakirah (8)
Barnes Junior School, Sunderland

The Adventure Of Ted And Bailey

One day, Ted and Bailey escaped from their homes and went on an adventure in Barnes Park. First, they found a raft and set out on the lake. When they reached the bridge, they got off. Then they found themselves lost - but Elizabeth had noticed so she set out for Barnes Park.

Eventually, Elizabeth found Ted and Bailey but they'd both seen a squirrel and ran after it. But Elizabeth got them on their leads. "Let's go back home," said Elizabeth. So they went back home and had their breakfast, just in time for the twins to play football.

Benjamin Poulton (8)
Barnes Junior School, Sunderland

How They Defeated The Dark

Evil was taking over good. The good gang decided they must bring good back. They only had until sunset. Their journey started at the Jumbo jungle, swinging from vine to vine over swamps. They jumped on crocodile heads to get across rivers. They arrived at Wonderland and asked the people where the Star of Light was. They pointed to the Rocky Road Mountain. The sun was setting so they ran up the mountain. They grabbed the Star and went home. As they arrived, they had seconds to climb the Monument to place it. The Star was placed and evil disappeared.

Lily Wardle (8)
Barnes Junior School, Sunderland

Lola Vs The Evil Sorcerer

As I entered the ancient, enchanted forest, I felt ecstatic. I was about to find the most magical bunny, that possesses every power in the universe. All of a sudden, there was a massive hurricane. I was petrified but, somehow, it stopped. Then emerged the most evil sorcerer in the world. She wanted to take over the Earth with the bunny's powers. But I wasn't about to let that happen! I started complimenting her and then I gave her a hug and she turned into black dust on the forest floor. Finally, I'd found her weakness. Always be kind!

Lola Cottee-Gohren (8)

Barnes Junior School, Sunderland

Lucy, Ben, And The Minotaur

There were two children called Lucy and Ben. A mysterious minotaur killed their parents, so they came back for revenge. They went into the mysterious forest and, before they knew it, they met the monster.

They saw a sword next to a tree. Lucy ran to recover it while Ben distracted the monster. Lucy came back with the sword and charged at the monster while Ben sneaked behind and got his knife that he used to protect himself. Lucy killed the minotaur with the sword. They could use his magical orb necklace to return back to their lovely house.

Lucia Phillips (8)

Barnes Junior School, Sunderland

Missing Parents

There once was a boy called Tim, he was on an adventure to find his parents. He had siblings called Janet and his brother was Lamby. They made a chicken, flying, rainbow vehicle. They had to go somewhere called Mount Olympus, so they packed their stuff and set off! When they got there, they climbed and climbed. They lost hope and climbed down their ladder and found their parents. When they were unfrozen, they thought they'd be happy they'd found the kids. They lost their vehicle and then two people came and saved them. Finally!

Autumn Elliott (9)
Barnes Junior School, Sunderland

The Adventures Of Bailey And Ted

Once upon a time, there were two dogs who bumped into each other in a forest. They announced their names to each other. The beige dog was Bailey, the grey dog was called Ted. They agreed to be friends. They met in the Forest of Doom. They came across a skeleton with a map in its chest. They took the map from the skeleton. They found a cave, they slept in it. On day two, Ted and Bailey woke up at 7:30. They found a golden statue waiting outside for them. Once Ted touched it, they fell into a cave!

Edward Paulton (8)
Barnes Junior School, Sunderland

Saffi's Birthday

One day, there was a girl named Saffi. She loved frogs and her birthday was on the 2nd December. She was turning nine tomorrow. That night, she went to bed and her dream was amusing. She left her house to look for frogs and she crossed a really choppy sea, rowed to the Amazon rainforest, and even ran from a snake. Finally, she got there but sadly she woke up. But was it a dream or not? Because when she woke up, she had the scar made in her dream! So she lived to wonder.

Saffi Johnson (9)
Barnes Junior School, Sunderland

The Night I Met An Elf

On the first day of Christmas, I got an elf. His name was Loui. My name is Elle and I am eight years old. Today, my elf, Loui, covered the whole house in tinsel. I wanted to find out how he did it so I woke up at midnight and sneaked downstairs to see if the elf was moving - he was! Then I got hold of him and asked how he did it. He said he had elf magic. I asked if I could have some and Loui said yes! From then on, we all lived happily ever after.

Emily Routledge (9)
Barnes Junior School, Sunderland

The Boy And The Abandoned House

At seven in the morning, I went out into my garden and found this door and went through it. I saw a house and a boy there. I asked him, "What's your name?"

The boy said, "What's yours?"

I said, "Kyle."

He said, "Jamie."

We explored. Jamie kept saying 'Bloody Mary'. When I turned back, he was next to me. We went into a dirty house, there was rum and Baileys there. We saw a shotgun, I took it.

We drank and Jamie got drunk and was going mad. I said, "Stop or I'm going to shoot you."

Jayvon Kyle Thompson (9)

Comber Grove School, London

The Girl Who Changed The Universe

Once upon a time, on January 1st 2001, asteroids came. Asteroids were destroying houses and life. So, six years later, came Harley Goldsburg. When Harley was young, her dad, Crowley Goldsburg, told her what was going on with the asteroids and how they were destroying lives. So she'd always been interested in asteroids, up to when she was sixteen. She decided to go on her computer to research about asteroids. On her computer, she found out that the planet that had been causing this was called Alibariba. She was so eager she created, after twelve months, a rocket.

Lyron Nai (9)
Comber Grove School, London

Crossing The Line

Once upon a time, there was a pair of twins, one boy and one girl. Their names were Ava and Arron. They and their parents lived in a small village next to the darkest forest. The twins' mother was deeply sick and their father didn't care at all. "We need to cross the border!" Arron would always try to plead with his father every day, but he always said no. One day, they crossed. Running through the forest, they found the cure, but Ava had passed out due to the pressure. As he ran home, they cured their mother!

Lanai Smith (9)
Comber Grove School, London

A Nightmare Come True

One night, I went to bed. I immediately went into a dream, well, a nightmare. My name is Sea and I'm a broken angel. I'm an angel mixed up with a demon. Like sun mixed with moon. Every night I go into this dream. I've been trying to escape but I can't.

Today is the day. I've got to use my powers so I can stop this dream from happening again. Well, I'll try.

"You must keep going," says a voice. Okay, one more time... what just happened? I can escape now! Hooray!

Mahalee Bryan (9)
Comber Grove School, London

Magic Boy

Once upon a time, there lived a boy called Jack.
One day, he woke up strangely and put his shoes
on and wandered around until he discovered a
spooky, dark forest. He took a step inside and,
from a distance, he saw a shining bright light so he
decided to walk to it, since he was bored. When he
got there, it sort of felt like a power in his body. As
soon as it happened, he heard someone saying,
"Help!" under a large rock. So he flew to it, lifted it
up, and he saved the person.

Djibril Ibrahima (9)
Comber Grove School, London

Lost On The Beach

While I was walking on the beach, I found a lost puppy and food. I was so hungry! There was a sandwich and mango juice. Then, later, I saw something moving in the trees so I went there to see and there it was - a giant, hungry tiger. I ran as fast as I could to not be eaten by an angry tiger! At 8PM I saw a man and the name of the man was Hayden. We said hello to each other. It started raining with lightning strikes. Then, on my phone, it said there was a tornado warning.

Luna Varela (10)
Comber Grove School, London

Once Upon A Time

Once upon a time, there was a boy called Discover. He was so good at imagining, so he shut his eyes and thought of a character.

He was called Billy. Billy was a boy. He had good grades and whatever he says, happens. So he thought, *what if I said, 'Give me magical powers'?* He said it to himself and it worked! He had the power to camouflage.

Discover opened his eyes and dinner was ready. So he went and never came back.

Seyma Erdal (9)
Comber Grove School, London

The Three Gifts

One day, Ava woke up to her phone and said hi to Amy and asked if she wanted to come over. Amy came with Emily and stayed for a while. Then Emily mistakenly knocked down a picture and found a code. She tried to unlock it and it worked. They found a crystal, in fact, two more. They looked inside them and it made them powerful. They decided to help people all over the world and be the best they could be.

Daniella Kamara Konday (10)
Comber Grove School, London

There's No Turning Back In NYC

There is no time. This world is going to be deserted. Our only saviour might be Mini Spider-Man. There are more than twenty villains out there already. All he has to do is break the portal... which is heavily guarded.

This is going to be intricate. He is not going to run away like a coward. He goes in and *boom!* The portal isn't destroyed, but his home is.

Aziz Kargbo (10)
Comber Grove School, London

The Paradise

On a sunny morning, me and my family were on a holiday in Hawaii with the kids, Jake and Ema.
"Kids, let's go to the pool."
"Max, honey, can you put sunscreen on the kids?" said Uma. "Wait, where are the kids' swimsuits?" said Uma.
"The swimsuits are in the blue bag," said Max.
"Let's go swim now, Mummy and Daddy."
"Okay. Cannonball!"
"Mum, you splashed us!"
"Sorry," said Uma.
"It's okay because we were going to do the same thing. Mum, let's have some ice cream and go back to the cabin to get undressed and into bed."

Rafaela Marques (9)
Elm Road Primary School, Wisbech

This Is

There I am, lying still, a car comes at me. I then wake, it's another time, I can't move... then there's a knife hitting my head.

Suddenly, I'm in my bed. Blood on my wall spells: *Deaths: 2.* I whimper many times before I fall back into a mini loop of torture - but this time I feel it.

A plane flies at me and hits my stationary corpse. Oh, that pain! I should've woke, but no. After five hundred deaths, I say, "Am I dead yet?"

There's a reply, "No, not yet."

"Who is this?"

"This is Requiem."

Deaths: infinite.

Ryan McCourt (10)

Elm Road Primary School, Wisbech

The Missing Children

Running from the rapidly flickering lights, a group of teenagers went inside the house. It was midnight, the door locked itself, they were stuck. They went into the closet. Footsteps were everywhere, lights were flickering, doors were opening. They'd never believed in ghosts until now. One friend fainted. Their flashlight flickered. They dropped it but it was still flickering. They were still hiding in the closet, then a knock on the closet door happened. It went harder and harder until one opened it and disappeared. It was weird. Another ran to open the door, he disappeared. The last escaped alone.

Alex Kosalka (11)
Elm Road Primary School, Wisbech

The House

A winter, dark and gloomy. There's a gem in a house. You can get anything you wish for. Lilly and Shopie see the house and enter it. A curtain flies through the room. A vampire is sitting there.

"What are you doing here?"

"I'm looking for a gem, have you seen it?"

"I have actually, it's upstairs." They walk upstairs and gas goes everywhere and they faint.

After a while, they wake up in a dungeon with monsters. A vampire, a witch, and a large beast say, "You're here for the gem, right? Bye-bye." And they won't be seen again...

Aleksandra Kontautaite (10)

Elm Road Primary School, Wisbech

Who Is It?

"We're here, I'm the murderer," I said. There were ten people there. I entered the abandoned house, everybody got there and the game started.
I followed Player 2 when everybody wasn't looking. I shot Player 2 with an NSP-S so no one would hear the gun. Someone reported the body. Player 3 screamed, "1 is the murderer!" and Player 1 was dead.
I made a titanic hole. I stayed with everybody, they were going to the hole. *I knew my plan would work*, I thought. Nearer and nearer I pushed them. They were screaming, I got my gun, shooting them...

Kevin Dilans (10)
Elm Road Primary School, Wisbech

Mermaids Help To Save People

One afternoon, I took a walk but, all of a sudden, I tripped. I thought I would fall on the ground but I didn't - I fell in a river. I thought I would drown but I didn't. I turned into a magical mermaid. I swam all day. Some fish needed my help.

"What's wrong?"

"Our friend is trapped in an old ship."

"I will help you save him. I like your fins."

"Yours too."

"Thanks."

"Come on, let's go."

"*Help! Help! In here!*"

"Okay, we're coming to you."

Phoebe Ashton (9)

Elm Road Primary School, Wisbech

The Submarine

The submarine descended, the crew had evacuated except one. "Where are the suits?" The submarine was shipwrecked right on a trench. He only had an hour.

The sand crumbled under the weight. Ten minutes left. "Finally, I found the suits." But it took fifteen minutes to put on, so he started now but then *bang!* The submarine fell into the trench. Now he needed to escape from the submarine.

"Finally, I put it on!" Then he realised, if he opened the door he would get crushed. Then, *crunch, crunch,* then *bang!* He was dead.

Majus Kucys (11)

Elm Road Primary School, Wisbech

A Close Call

The colossal, sentient mountain overlooked the forest-filled valley. Nathan stepped foot onto the alien landscape. He tiptoed toward the valley. Nathan paused. Something was stalking him. He walked closer. A dark silhouette appeared, this turned out to be an alien. Nathan ran. The sinister alien chased him. He didn't want to be alien food. Was this the end? Was Nathan going to die? Nathan screeched. The devilish alien was close. As a last resort, he got out his blowtorch. The alien ran away in pain and fear.

"That was a close call," sighed Nathan.

Amir Afifi (10)
Elm Road Primary School, Wisbech

Jack And The Dragon

Jack was in a plane. Because of a crash that'd happened about five minutes ago, he just woke up from being knocked out. Then a voice said, coming out of nowhere, "Take this apple but use it wisely. For you have one chance on this."
Jack was confused. Then, out of nowhere, a gigantic dragon came charging at the plane! Jack suddenly knew what to do. He ate the apple. He felt stronger. He pulled the door off its hinges. He pushed the dragon out of the air. It blasted purple smoke, which didn't hurt. He'd broken the dragon's curse.

Gabriel Cleverly (8)
Elm Road Primary School, Wisbech

Exploring A Volcano

Tobiasz and I were exploring a jungle and we found a volcano. So we started to explore. We started to climb. We found an entrance, it was warm inside. We found a lava staff. I picked it up and we heard a roar. "What was that?" said Tobiasz.

We explored deeper - it was a lava monster. I used the staff to create rocks to trap the lava monster. The lava monster broke out. I started to summon rocks and threw them at the lava monster. The lava monster exploded. The volcano started to erupt. We rushed out of the volcano.

Dylan Gant (8)
Elm Road Primary School, Wisbech

Halloween Night

On Halloween night, a group of three friends went trick-or-treating. One of the girls saw an abandoned house. Everyone wasn't sure if they wanted to go in, but they did. The door opened. They went in. A floor plank creaked. The trio got goosebumps but they continued.
One of them saw a strange handprint. It was too late to go back. The door shut. They started screaming for their lives. Meanwhile, they saw a rocking chair rocking itself.
They were reported missing. Their parents never saw them again.

Kalina Topalova (10)
Elm Road Primary School, Wisbech

The Escape Room

Kai tried to escape the white escape room. It had patterns on the ceiling, it looked like clouds. Kai pondered where he was but then he heard a *whoosh* noise and green, poisonous gas poured out of a pipe in the wall. Kai panicked, he scrambled around the room. He found a typewriter and saw an air vent on the side of the room. It was too high. Kai typed in random words on the typewriter. Nothing happened. He typed *help* and a staircase opened. He made it to the vent. He burst it open and escaped.

Jaiden Fabela (10)
Elm Road Primary School, Wisbech

The Temple

Tom stepped onto a bridge that was falling. The door was behind the waterfall. Something was rustling in the bushes. There was smoke in the distance. Tom entered the temple. When he walked into the temple, he saw it - the treasure. But to get it, he had to go through the traps. He quickly went through the traps and got the treasure. When Tom went back to the door, it wouldn't open. He was trapped! The only way to get out was by climbing through the top. He tried to climb but fell into the traps and died.

Nedas Jankauskas (11)
Elm Road Primary School, Wisbech

The Broken Stone

The floor rumbles. I'm covered in sweat, this island has the ancient stone. Unfortunately, it is guarded by tribe men. I know where it is because it is marked on my map.

I finally reach the destination. I dash past the tribe men, getting scratched in the process. The sand gets in my eyes. Although in pain, I still open my eyes. I grab hold of the stone but I feel a sharp pain in my back. I kneel in pain. The stone shatters, it loses colour. I start fainting and then it all turns pitch-black.

Raivo Mazurs (11)
Elm Road Primary School, Wisbech

The Spies

A long time ago, me and my mates became spies but we had an imposter in the group. I needed to activate the portal but it was disabled because the imposter broke it. So me and the spies found parts to fix it. We continued to look for blood evidence but somebody died. I called a meeting. We ran to the centre while getting chased by the imposter. I shut the door on the imposter. It was Green Agent. After the meeting, we all went to find parts again. Then we found all the parts and went into the portal.

Danielius Morling (8)
Elm Road Primary School, Wisbech

The Haunted House

Sofie had some courage so she went outside to see where the lady went, but she was not to be found. Then Sofie went back inside and went to sleep. She woke up in a haunted house, she was trapped in a room.

Then a voice said, "Do a puzzle and you will be set free."

So she did what the voice said and completed the puzzle and escaped and ran outside. Then she woke up terrified but she knew it was a dream. So she went downstairs and relaxed and got the dream out of her tired head.

Emilija Krukonyte (8)

Elm Road Primary School, Wisbech

Exploring An Enormous Volcano

Me and Dylan went into a very overgrown forest and we found a scorching-hot volcano. We went to explore it. We started to climb, then we found an entrance. It was very warm inside and Dylan picked up a lava star.

Then we heard a roar and said, "What was that?" We explored but it was a lava monster. Then me and Dylan split up and went in different directions. We took a big stone and kept throwing it until he was defeated. Me and Dylan said, "We're never coming back."

Tobiasz Bardzinski-Konczynski (8)
Elm Road Primary School, Wisbech

The End

As a wailing scream comes down the road, I took a peek at the midnight sky out the window, to see a narrow house. I walked up to the crooked house, the doors creaked open, taking my first step as goosebumps coiled my body. The door creaked open, swinging by itself, but it was just me. I rushed upstairs and, in an old suitcase, I find a map to the missing princess. I leapt to the back garden and started to dig. I pulled up the bones and realised that this was the last part of the lost princess.

Maizie Hopson (10)
Elm Road Primary School, Wisbech

The Secret Lake

I'm on a quest to see if the secret lake is real. I jump in. My eyes, what is wrong with them? I tell myself, "Don't be scared." Help. Nothing is happening. I open my eyes and I see a door. "Where am I?" I look around and it's an old house. It's stinky, scary, and I don't want to be here. I open the door and I'm in the sky. Nothing's here and I look down - it's high. Someone pushes me and I'm holding on for my life. I fall...

Ethan Foster (11)
Elm Road Primary School, Wisbech

Jane The Mysterious Mermaid

Hello, my name is Jane Coper and I am a mermaid. Everyone has been talking about this mysterious, underwater land but no one has been there yet. I really want to go there but I need to solve some mysteries. I found a rock with some writing on it. It said: *Everyone can see you but they can't see me, and it is on something big.* So I've figured out a rock, a big rock. So I go over there but I go under the rock and I find the mysterious land! I take all of the treasure.

Daniele Binkulyte (9)
Elm Road Primary School, Wisbech

The Haunted House

It's a cold night in the winter. A wooden house with boards on its windows is waiting there for me to explore. The door creaks open, someone or something is behind me but I am just too blind to see it. I look, there isn't anything there. I turn my torch on but it goes out in the blink of an eye. I hear an explosion, the ground rumbles and I hear a scream. I run. But I know I have to save them, whoever it is, I have to save them. I walk through the hallway. Bye-bye, world.

Caitlan Simper (10)
Elm Road Primary School, Wisbech

Ivor's Short Adventure

As I stepped in, the door cracked open. I heard the creature roar right in my ears. As I stepped out, the roaring stopped. My name is Ivor and I was there to fight dragons, get eggs, and find their secrets. I heard breathing behind me. I grabbed my sword and stared. I turned around and it was a dragon. I cut it until I found an egg. It was a great catch - an earth dragon! I went and got nearly to the end, but nothing. I got tired. Then I saw a bed so I got in and slept.

Odeta Glinskaja (8)
Elm Road Primary School, Wisbech

Abandoned House

The lights were flickering like lightning in the sky. The floorboards were creaking. It smelled damp. I could see broken windows at every angle, I could hear the alarms going off to warn the police. When I entered the haunted mansion, it was so spooky. I could feel someone touching me on the shoulders... I could also hear the door opening. I could see the shadows of everything in the haunted house. Suddenly, I could hear a huge, *boo!* The piano was playing by itself.

Maisie Brighty (11)
Elm Road Primary School, Wisbech

Abandoned House

It's a cold, dark night and, as I enter the house, I get a cold chill. There is a light flickering in the other room, so I go near it. All of a sudden it goes dark, so I leave the room. A shadow runs past me and I light my torch. I go upstairs, following the light. I never think about going into the bedroom but, when I do, I see a light. It's golden. When I get near to the door, it slams closed. My torch goes out. I enter the bathroom and, suddenly, there it is...

Emilia Jones (11)
Elm Road Primary School, Wisbech

Haunted House

Spooky sounds came from the house. Lights flickered when I entered and, all of a sudden, I heard a big bang from the basement. The lights turned off and I went down, curious. A shadow ran past me. I lit my torch and tiptoed further toward the shadows. I saw a hanging candle and I pulled it. The wall made a doorway and then I entered. I saw a light shine coming from the attic. I had to find a ladder. There was one in the cupboard. I climbed it. There it was, the treasure.

Harry Hobbs (10)
Elm Road Primary School, Wisbech

Zeus And Zeus' Lightning Bolt

I was on a mission to use the mythical Zeus' thunderbolt that could set people on fire excruciatingly. I was going to use it to give people free electricity and set bad people on fire so there were only good people on the planet. Now I went to the mountain. After a few days, I finally made it to the mountain. I went to talk to Zeus. I told him why I needed it and he gave me it. Now I was going to make all people that were bad gone, and give people free electricity.

Danielius Janulis (8)
Elm Road Primary School, Wisbech

In The Maze

In the maze, I was walking, trying to get my way out, then I heard all of the creepiest noises. Like a sheep, loudly. As I walked a bit faster because that noise was so creepy, there were two turnings. Which way should I go? Left or right? Oh, there's a mummy! Think. Right! Run!
A minute later, I was fine. I got away. I fell over, well that hurt. I kept walking and crows surrounded me and tried to get me. Something landed on me - a key to get out of there.

Jaiden Bird (10)
Elm Road Primary School, Wisbech

The Dragon

I opened a glowing box and there was a baby dragon inside. I picked it up. The dragon had a boy part, it was a boy. He was blue and red so, when he grew up, he'd be able to control water and fire. Five minutes later, I'd named him Ben. Ben jumped out of my hands and hid. I tried to find him but I couldn't see him. It didn't help that we were in the jungle. But then I ran because I saw him drinking from the river. I ran over there so, so fast.

Alexis Bampton (9)
Elm Road Primary School, Wisbech

The Cursed Box

Once upon a time, there was a cursed box that if you dared to open it, you would be cursed. So, let me tell you the full story.

There was a boy called Max, his dream was to find the cursed box. One day, Max went out to the jungle and he was going to find the box. As he was going, he ran out of water. Before he gave up, he saw a mysterious temple. He found the box and opened it and he discovered a superpower. But a cursed body beat him up, but he won.

Bamidele Olawoye (8)
Elm Road Primary School, Wisbech

Mysterious Lake

I walk up to the mysterious lake and its night. I grab my conical flask and my DNA stick. The colour of the lake is a murky green. I feel a gust of wind coming to me. As I stick my DNA stick into the river, the water splashes me, it's warm.
The wind gets rougher. I can see something swirling in the distance. It gets closer to me. *Whoosh*, the wind hits me. I lose my conical flask, and the sample I collected changed me today.

Emilis Darguzas (10)
Elm Road Primary School, Wisbech

The Ocean

I was at the beach. I was swimming until I saw a glowing box on a shipwreck. So I swam down. The closer I got, the worse the water got. I was so close to grabbing the box until a whirlpool appeared and it sucked me to the top of the ocean. I was so mad, I was that close to the box and I just got sucked right to the top so many times after that. I got nowhere near the box so I decided to give up and go back to my house.

Daniel Simper (8)
Elm Road Primary School, Wisbech

The Secret Superpower

One day, at 8:07PM, Olivia, who was eight, appeared to be in a jungle. Her friend, Max, felt petrified because he never knew if they would get lost or not.

"Max, I wanna explore the world! And be talented!" Olivia said.

"Okay, so what do you want to do to make it come true?" Max said.

"Huh!" Olivia cried.

"Why are you saying 'Huh'?" Max replied.

"Look over there! It's a... a..." She was lost for words. There it was, an extraordinary, gloomy bottle. On the bottle it said: *The Secret Superpower*.

"Drink it!" Max screamed. So she did!

Daisy Groom (9)
Holtsmere End Junior School, Woodhall Farm

A Mystery To Solve

Once, a little girl was in a jungle. But it wasn't an ordinary jungle, no! It was called the Jungle of Mystery. Let it begin!

"Wow, this mystery is hard. Aha! I found a note," said Maiya. She couldn't read it so she took it to the Mayor.

"Hm, it says: *I'll be back*. But, him? Not Harry?" She saw Harry walking and she said, "Hey, Harry, you're mean!"

"Fine, it was me. I was the mean boy who bullied you but I'm sorry, will you forgive me?"

"Yes." And they became friends and the pair were never mean again!

Grace Groom (7)
Holtsmere End Junior School, Woodhall Farm

Mission Of The Golden Crystal

When two girls went walking in a field near their house, they would have never been prepared for what was coming next. As they walked under the sparkling stars, a woman with a slender figure and bedraggled clothes ran up to them, handed them a glowing, amber-ish crystal, and said, "You two will become us. Travel the mountains, oceans, deserts, and forests." She smiled while another woman appeared beside her, and they both faded into the shadows.

The young girls realised wolves had been chasing the women. Dashing home, they packed all they needed and left for their future.

Amy Diggines (11)
Holtsmere End Junior School, Woodhall Farm

The Opal

There was once a castle in Scotland named Loch Gem. In the great Loch, there were eight princesses: Sapphire, Ruby, Emerald, Gold, Silver, Diamond, Crystal, and the youngest one, Opal. Each princess had a crystal representing their name, but one was missing - and it was Opal's. The opal was located in a cave thousands of miles away. Knights with gleaming swords failed to acquire it because their ship sank like the Titanic. Five people managed to return the opal to the palace and they were all rewarded. Young Opal then received her jewel and the Princess was happily welcomed.

Andreea Abunei (9)
Holtsmere End Junior School, Woodhall Farm

The Future

Once, long ago, there was a girl named Sunflower. She had a mum and dad but, one day, her father, Nico, never came back. Two years later, Kyle was born. Five years later, Sunflower found a glowing key under her bed that took her to the past. Kyle followed Sunflower.

Nico said, "This is my daughter, Sunflower, and my wife will be upset."

"I know, Nico, but we need you."

"So that's why Dad never came home, he's captured."

"We need to go and save him." So they saved their dad and they lived happily ever after.

Antonina Grygiel (9)

Holtsmere End Junior School, Woodhall Farm

Ice Quest

One stormy and cold morning, Luke woke up, finding an amethyst shard. He'd heard about these before. On the amethyst, it said: *Retrieve the map that lurks within the coldness.* Within a second, he was in the frost and coldness.

In the distance was the ice castle. He knew that was a good sign. He looked through the window and inside was a cold piece of paper, so he knew it was there. He entered without fear and walked up the stairs. An icicle fell near him. "*Ahh!*" he screamed. So he dashed and grabbed the map.

Oliver Potter (9)
Holtsmere End Junior School, Woodhall Farm

The Magic Penguin

Once upon a time a cute little penguin named Lily went out exploring on a scary but slow walk. She saw a little dragon. The dragon was really kind, he went with the penguin. On the way, they found lots of magical creatures, like a werewolf, mermaid, and a galaxy dog as well.

Lilly walked with all her new friends, but felt left out because she didn't have any powers. So she carried on walking, all sad. Then it happened, they reached the palace. She rushed inside, when she came out, she was a sparkling magical penguin and lived happily.

Stella French (9)

Holtsmere End Junior School, Woodhall Farm

The Gem Hunt

Once upon a time, there was a witch called Mrs Kianso. She was a gloomy woman who never really interacted with the public. People described her as an odd woman who caused no harm.

One mysterious day, she received a letter: *You have an hour to receive the gem. If you don't, Earth will be destroyed.* She gasped in fear but she knew there was no time to lose. She got up with her black boots. Suddenly, there was a huge shake. Shockingly, she realised she had a minute left. She took action quickly and raced to the empty cell.

Abby Thapa (8)
Holtsmere End Junior School, Woodhall Farm

The Lost Jungle

Suddenly, I awoke in the middle of nowhere. I was confused. Why, or where, was I? Then I realised I was in an ever-blooming, evergreen jungle. I stood. I was peacefully lying on the muddy tropical floor. After, I saw a mark on one of the rocks. It said: *The mist covers old so fast unless the truth comes alive.* Then I saw a trapdoor. I went into it. Cautiously, I went around every corner. I was feeling courageous. With a few steps, I saw a magical crystal. I decided to touch it, slowly. Swiftly, I could magically teleport.

Melissa Stefanoaia (9)
Holtsmere End Junior School, Woodhall Farm

How To Break A Curse

The magical key glowed and took us on a journey and then we met a person. I didn't know their name. But then I knew the way to go to break the curse. Then the person came to help me but he told me his name was Harry.
I said, "Oh, that's your name."
"But I didn't like it," said Harry Potter. "I was like, 'Noo'. I hated the name."
We found a curse but we tried to the code. We all managed to break it. We found another curse, we tried to break it, but it had a code.

Skye Kennie (11)
Holtsmere End Junior School, Woodhall Farm

Toilet Quest

I went to the bathroom but the keys dropped and fell in the toilet!

I was sucked in there too!

"*Level One*," a deep voice said. That's when I noticed that I was now in the sewer!

Crocodiles and huge rats tried to eat me, so I ran like lightning. Then a shark jumped in the air like a dolphin and tried to eat me.

I ran with all my might and was covered with bruises. I leapt into the air and screamed, "*Aahh!*" Then I heard a jingle, it was the keys!

And I woke up.

Uthman Fatih (10)

Holtsmere End Junior School, Woodhall Farm

The Magical Curse

Once, in a rainforest, there lived two girls called Amy and Jess who discovered a superpower that was reading minds! There was a curse upon them which they knew about, it was their superpowers that they just discovered with the curse.
So they went to a kingdom to break it, but to break it they would have to do something in return. So they had to fight Agent Nero! So both of them fought him and won. Nero was so afraid, he asked them to break the curse. So their superpowers disappeared and they lived happily ever after.

Aanya Chandarana (8)
Holtsmere End Junior School, Woodhall Farm

Cufty And The Everlasting Leaf

The once was a beautiful fluffy caterpillar called Cufty and he was almost always hungry. One day, he went to find more food. He ate: Christmas trees, candy canes, flowers, mince pies, breadcrumbs, and gingerbread men. Looking for that was really hard to do! But he did it.

He then decided to find the everlasting leaf. He ate and ate to be ready for the long journey. He went across fire hills and then he built a raft to go over the ocean. He then got to the plains of the field and he found it - the everlasting leaf!

Ryan Gay (9)
Holtsmere End Junior School, Woodhall Farm

Oliver's Adventure

Oliver knew the disappearance of his friend was down to the witch. All that was left of Harry was purple dust. He knew he had no time to waste, and the only way to get him back was to destroy the witch's wand. Oliver grabbed his sword and ran as fast as he could to where the witch would be waiting.

As he entered her small hut, screams were heard. Cautiously, he walked towards her. He clenched his sword and struck the wicked witch. She fell to the ground and purple dust came out of her mouth. What just happened?

James Hart (11)

Holtsmere End Junior School, Woodhall Farm

The Magical Illness

Once, in a kingdom, there lived a King and Queen. One day, the Queen had babies, their names were Amy and Milly. After that, she was ill. Only one thing could make her better, only a golden flower. Milly and Amy set off to find the golden flower. The golden flower was located in a farmer's field. The farmer was crazy. He would eat you if you stole the flower. Milly and Amy found the flower but the farmer found them. But the farmer was really nice! Milly and Amy went home and gave the flower to their mother.

Lily-Alice Stiff (9)
Holtsmere End Junior School, Woodhall Farm

The Diamond Saviour

In the freezing snow, Lola ran with all her might. She checked her watch, she had only ten minutes to retrieve the diamond from the cave. She knew what she needed to do, since this was her sweet twin, Lila. Five minutes left on the clock and Lola almost fainted. Extremely weak, with two minutes left on the timer, Lola had the diamond! She knew that Uncle would have to give back Lila now. She called him on her emergency phone with no hesitation. As soon as he saw the diamond, he released Lila and all was well again.

Millie Beamon (11)

Holtsmere End Junior School, Woodhall Farm

The Lost Key And The City

I heard a voice, it said, "You, Charlotte, have a year to find a lost key and find the hole that the key fits, to find a lost city."

I said, "Yes, of course, I will do it." So the next day, I went looking for the key. After three months, I found the key. I felt surprised. A neon, red button was at the back of the forest, it had the words: *Don't Push!*

Suddenly, I pushed the button. It opened a gate, so I put the key into it and it led me to the wonderful lost city!

Charlotte Mitchell (9)
Holtsmere End Junior School, Woodhall Farm

The Galaxy Queen

Once upon a time, there lived a girl called Sky. She lived in a house with her parents.

One day they passed away but left her a letter, to get her powers she had to go to the moon.

She got a job and went on a rocket. She was excited. She finally got to the moon.

When they landed she ran off straight away. When she looked back she saw they had left her. Puzzled she realised she had powers, so skipped back to Earth.

When she passed away, in her honour, they gave her a big statue.

T'iarah Bowen (8)
Holtsmere End Junior School, Woodhall Farm

Dora And The Swiping Swiper

Dora had a school trip. Their class was going to the woods. Then, when they got there, Dora found a dog who led them into a cold, dark, and grey cave. There was a sign that said: *Do Not Enter.* Dora, being an eleven-year-old, went into the cave. As she went in, she saw a bed with wet sheets. She saw Swiper, the guy that wanted to swipe the whole world away. She began to get her sword and slay him, but he dodged. Then she snapped her fingers, then she snapped the world away.

Nelly Wheller (10)
Holtsmere End Junior School, Woodhall Farm

Zombie Treasure

One day, Donut Man asked his friend to go to find treasure. They went. Ten minutes later, they were there. The car broke. The car crashed on a rock. There was a water fountain and there was a river across the mountain. A zombie came and then got a superpower. More came. They ran and ran and ran until they found treasure. But the zombies came. One hundred came. They were scared but it was daytime so the zombies didn't like light. So they got the treasure and left. They got back home.

Logan Wallace (8)

Holtsmere End Junior School, Woodhall Farm

Searching For Gold

Once upon a time, there was someone called Alex who was a poor person. He got a metal detector for his birthday. He went to the woods every day but none of them were successful so he gave up. He didn't go for ages.

One day, he tried it out for the first time that year. Alex was thirteen now and decided to go and search for gold. It took him four hours to find four pots of pure gold. He was excited and they were heavy, so he called his dad to bring his car to help.

Iraklis Karamitsos (8)
Holtsmere End Junior School, Woodhall Farm

How I Broke The Curse

I had until sunset to find the Princess and break the curse that the wicked witch put on her. I was furious at the witch because she transformed the Princess into a tree in a rainforest. It took me a while to figure out that I had to pull a leaf out of the tree to break the spell. The deserted forest was very scary but I managed to reach the leaf before it got dark. The Princess took me to live with her in her ancient castle.

Sara Stevlik (7)
Holtsmere End Junior School, Woodhall Farm

The Mystery Murder

"What is that?" I said as I noticed a shiny sparkle coming from Katie's wardrobe.

"I think you should go," she said nervously.

I left and drove home. I examined my notes to track the thief. I studied the case and found no more information. The next morning, I drove to the police station and I got a phone call.

"Help! Someone is in my house!" she said in a petrified tone.

I ran to the crime scene and saw a body lying there, unconscious. "I found the weapon!" I shouted proudly. I examined the fingerprints, gasping, "It was Katie!"

Charlotte Bianchi (11)
New Monkland Primary School, Glenmavis

The Beginning Of The Quest To Find A Magic Chicken

I woke up early. The day had begun. It was time to do it. Flashing back to yesterday, at first an ordinary day, I was on a walk when a woman came up to me and started yelling. She was telling me I'd been chosen. I told her to calm down and tell me what was happening.
She said, "You have to catch a loose... chicken!"
"A loose chicken? Really?" I replied. I wanted to know what was so important about this chicken.
She said, "It's a very magical chicken."
I had to think about it. "It's a deal."

Mollie Chaddock (10)
New Monkland Primary School, Glenmavis

The Abandoned Village

On December 14th 1976, two little boys went on a walk around the street in an abandoned village. It was frosty and cold, so they were wrapped up with scarves, hats, and gloves. The little boys were named Michael and Noah. They were walking in silence, looking around.

Noah stopped in shock, looking in the window. Michael looked up in curiosity and he froze. Something was looking down at them from the window upstairs. The boys blinked and it disappeared. They went inside and saw it at the top of the stairs. It was a ghost that was trapped inside.

Freya Blair (11)
New Monkland Primary School, Glenmavis

The Worst Robber In The World

One night a guy called Michael decided to rob a jewellery store, he was mainly focusing on the Rolexes.

So as he went over to the counter his elbow accidentally pressed the emergency button off. He grabbed some Rolex watches, quickly 'jumped' over the counter and ran out of the shop.

When Michael reached his hideout spot he started to check the Rolex watches 'BUT' just at that moment Michael got raided by police.

At the end Michael got sentenced to five years in jail for his actions, he's learnt his lesson.

Sufyaan Sharif (11)
New Monkland Primary School, Glenmavis

The Wild Wild West

I only had until sunset to complete my task, or I would be trapped here forever. The wild west was exciting but not somewhere I wanted to be trapped. I had to work quickly to find my brother and bring him home to our time.

I reluctantly walked into the nearest building and felt a strange feeling in my stomach. Something wasn't right. It felt like there were people watching me, but there was none in there. I felt something run its fingers through my hair. I realised that this place might be haunted. How would I save my brother?

Lola Hunt (11)

New Monkland Primary School, Glenmavis

The Curse Of Dust

'Ghosts don't exist'. Then what was that? I walked up the eerie, cracked stairs to find out where the noise was coming from. It was coming from the old, 1800s bedroom. I opened the door and there was a glowing ghost in the middle of the room. I couldn't believe it. It was so bright. I reached out and put my hand through its body. It felt so weird. Suddenly, I felt something fall on my head. The ghost said I had twenty-four hours to live and then I would fade away. I couldn't believe what I was hearing.

Ellie McFarland (10)
New Monkland Primary School, Glenmavis

The Truth Of Hook

The pirates had heard a curious rumour about Hook. They looked at the map, then at each other, and set sail to find Hook and interrogate him. They were halfway across the bay when they saw Hook's ship. They caught up with his ship and captured him.

They threw him in an empty cell, asked him multiple times, and finally found out that he was a previous Lost Boy, but that he gave up and grew up. The rumours had been true. This shocked all of the pirates, but they agreed to never speak of the situation again.

Rudy Wood (11)
New Monkland Primary School, Glenmavis

The Wanted Friend

One night, I was chilling upstairs and figuring out what my job would be, but I heard something downstairs. When I went down, there was nobody inside and the door was open. I went outside and I saw a poster about my friend. *I know, I am going and I'll try to find the truth about the post.*
I ran upstairs, searching the room for the truth. Then my friend came out of my closet. I ran away to call the cops but he was too fast.
He got me and trapped me in my room and said, "Goodnight."

Mitchell Scott Manson (11)
New Monkland Primary School, Glenmavis

Bright Light In Olanah

Today, I woke up not in my bed but in a cave. It was dark, smelly, and freezing. I saw a bright purple light looming in front of me. I was so curious to find out what it was, so I started walking toward it. The cave went black again.

In the blink of an eye, a hand reached out, grabbed me, and pulled me through a portal. I was petrified. This brings me to where I am right now: Planet Olanah.

You probably won't believe me, but there is some kind of creature watching me. It's coming! Send help!

Kara Beggs (11)
New Monkland Primary School, Glenmavis

They Are Here

I was petrified. They were here, all around. I couldn't escape the car I was in. I couldn't see them but I couldn't look. I knew I couldn't. I'd go crazy if I did. What could I do? I whimpered so they couldn't hear me. They'd taken everyone, excluding my family. I was by myself, so I tried to think of a plan. I'd wait five minutes, move from car to car and go into any open house I saw. That was my plan! Let's go. I moved from car to car to get to a house that was unlocked.

Holly McDougall (11)
New Monkland Primary School, Glenmavis

Finding The Truth

I was having a clear-out in my house this morning when I found a weird letter in my attic. It said: *If you ever find this letter, I'm watching you everywhere you go.* I shivered. I'd never felt so scared in my life.

"Wait, what if there are cameras in my house?" I said aloud. I was petrified. I heard my doorbell go. I checked and there was a strange man at my door. I ran out of my back door as fast as I could until I saw something that would change my life forever and ever...

Olivia Brownlie (11)
New Monkland Primary School, Glenmavis

Willow The Giant Dog

I had loved my dog ever since I got her. Her name was Willow and she was a very lively cockapoo. But, one day, something happened that would change my life forever. I was playing with Willow in my back garden, tossing her ball around. She was chasing it like a happy dog when the neighbours next door threw a blueberry muffin over the fence. I rushed over but Willow beat me to it and took a big bite out of the muffin. I thought she would be okay but then Willow let out a deafening bark and started growing!

Evan McAuley (11)
New Monkland Primary School, Glenmavis

The Cave Rescue

We had to get out of there. Faster and faster, closer and closer. We had to keep the necklace or they would be trapped in there forever. Who would be trapped forever, you ask? Jemima, Tom, and Reece, my best friends. The baddies were Ben and Jim. Ben and Jim put a curse on Jemima, Tom, and Reece, and the necklace would save them.
I had 'til sunset to set them free. I was looking back to see where they were and, the next thing I knew, I was unconscious and trapped with Jemima, Tom and Reece. No!

Lauren McKennan (10)
New Monkland Primary School, Glenmavis

The Scary Adventure

One day, I was on an adventure with my friend and we heard a strange noise coming from the woods. We reluctantly decided to go in and investigate. Each step was scarier than the last, but nothing was to be seen.

We went deeper into the woods. Suddenly, there was a bang. I stood still for one whole minute, holding my breath, and then I ran. The sound of footsteps was getting louder behind us. I was really starting to regret going on this adventure. How would we escape this?

Evie Hutton (11)

New Monkland Primary School, Glenmavis

The Quest To Find The Girl

One morning, I woke up and found a letter sitting on my bed. I opened it up to see what it said, and found instructions to go on a quest and save someone. But I only had until sunset. I didn't know who I was saving but I knew I had to go.
I got dressed in comfy clothes because I didn't know what the weather would be like. I grabbed the enclosed map. I walked and walked but no sign of them. I heard a few noises but couldn't see anything. Then, all of a sudden...

Skye Young (11)
New Monkland Primary School, Glenmavis

The Glowing Box

"Nanny, what's the box doing?"

"Open it!"

Okay... *ahh!*" says Olivia, being lifted up.

"Now you have powers to save the world. Go, save it!"

"Okay." Olivia flies away.

"You! How are you flying?"

"I'm saving the world!"

"Well, I'm your villain."

"Err, okay. When?"

"Now!"

Olivia gets ready to battle. Ready, set, go! Olivia and the villain fight for hours, but Olivia finally uses her super-strength to throw him into space.

"Hi, Mum and Dad, I just defeated a villain, became a millionaire, and now I'm watching telly!"

"Cool, Olivia."

Suddenly, the villain appears for a big rematch.

Niamh Murphy (8)
Pheasey Park Farm Primary School, Great Barr

Marsh, Mellow, Pop And Corn Defeat Lumo

One day, Marsh woke up and saw a diamond on the floor. On it, it said *Pop and Corn* and was full of black. "Mellow, come and look!"
"What is it, Marsh?" asked Mellow.
"We must smash it!" They smashed it and out flew Pop and Corn!
"Hi, Marsh and Mellow! Lumo has tried to make us evil again!" said Pop.
"Where is he?" asked Marsh.
"There!" moaned Corn.
"Marsh! Mind control!"
"Sorry! Three, two, one, mind control! Now, Lumo, explode yourself!" shouted Marsh.
"Okay, master." *Boom!*
"Yes! We did it!" they all screamed.
"Pop and Corn, live with us!"

Leah Wacogne (8)
Pheasey Park Farm Primary School, Great Barr

Wolfy And Tio

"It started when I created the group," said Willow. Willow walked to Katie. "Hi Katie, have you heard about the infection?"

"No, Willow."

"Ugh, useless cat." Willow appeared in a black place with portals.

"Hello, Willow. I know the infection," said a random voice.

"Who are you? How do you know me?" asked Willow.

"I'm not telling, but if you want a cure, go to Lucella Lab," said the voice.

Willow set off to the lab. "I'm finally here!" Willow saw one infected and worried. Willow heard a voice.

"I'm Tio!" said the mystery voice. Willow turned into a member!

Grayson Franklin (8)
Pheasey Park Farm Primary School, Great Barr

Henry And Charlie's Adventure

We had to go across the rapids so we could get to the portal. "We need to jump across the river!"

"I have to if you can't, jump!" I was glad we both made it.

"Look at all these dinosaurs."

"Stop getting distracted! Let's find this gem." That might take a while.

"I will have to go this way and you'll have to go that way."

"What if we get lost?"

"God help us then." Hopefully we wouldn't get lost because this gem was really important.

"Wait, I see the cave."

"Grab the gem then! Thank you."

"We found it!"

Henry Newey (8)
Pheasey Park Farm Primary School, Great Barr

The Christmas Dilemma

On a snowy day in the North Pole, Santa was getting ready for the big night - Christmas eve! He fed the reindeer and put their jingle bells on the side of their coats. Suddenly, there was a large bang. *Thud!* It was Kate and Maicie in the shed. "Santa!" cried Kate.

"Oh, hello Kate."

Maicie secretly picked up some snow to wrap it into a ball. She threw it at Santa. "Haha!"

"Maicie!" shouted Kate. Santa started to laugh. Suddenly, there was another bang. *Thud! Thud!* Kate checked outside - it was a giant, scary monster!

"*Aahh!*"

"I'll get it!"

Maicie Lees (9)
Pheasey Park Farm Primary School, Great Barr

Polar Save Santa

"One, two, three."

"Aha, I told you. Three seconds until the marshmallow goes down!" said Tom. It was a relief, getting away from home so he could get to see Saint Nicholas. I mean, Santa.

"Hop to bed, Tom," said Harry.

So Tom went to bed. Then there was a man under his bed! "Santa!" said Tom.

"Ho, ho, help me!" said Santa sadly.

"Right!" said Tom. So he freed Santa.

"What is going on? Get out, both of you."

So they went out and said together, "Merry Christmas, you're my hero." Then they just giggled and giggled.

Lola-rose Wheeldon
Pheasey Park Farm Primary School, Great Barr

Jay And The Mystery Of The Beasts

Why was there a jewel in his room? "What is that?" Jay asked. He was confused. Suddenly, a sky-blue mist glowed from the jewel. "I've got to touch it," he said.

He touched it. Suddenly, he teleported. "Where am I?" he asked.

"You're in Avantia," a voice said.

"Wizard Aduro?" he whispered.

"Yes, it's me. Quick, I need to give you a precious belt," Aduro said. Aduro gave him a belt that had elements.

So Jay set off. He kept walking and walking. "I need to defeat this beast," he said. Suddenly, he had found the majestic beast.

Solomon Georgiou (9)
Pheasey Park Farm Primary School, Great Barr

Save Christmas

Thud! In a faraway town, there were three girls. One of them, called Abigail looked out the window and saw something glowing from the distance. The girl woke up the others and told them what she saw, they all rushed down. There were tingles and booms. "*Aah!* What's that?" yelled Abigail. "It looks like Santa!" mysteriously whispered Amelia. Santa didn't have a red suit he had a green suit. Instead of going Ho Ho Ho he has a cackling laugh. The girls weren't scared, they started yelling at him. His ears were hurt so he dashed away. "Hooray, Christmas saved!"

Abigail Baingana (8)
Pheasey Park Farm Primary School, Great Barr

The Spy Ninja

There was once a man called Jonny. He was a spy and he saw an evil ninja so he followed him into the lab and heard him say, "This evil ninja machine is going to work and no one can stop me!"

"Oh, well I can, can't I?"

"Who are you, spy?"

"I'm Jonny."

"No you're not."

"Oh yes, I am. And I am the one that will destroy the machine."

"But you can only catch me *or* get the machine."

"I can get you first and then I can come back here and get the machine."

Theo Dwyer (8)

Pheasey Park Farm Primary School, Great Barr

Finding The Truth

One day, twins Faith and Noah were strolling on the beach. All of a sudden, they were getting drawn into the sea! Then... *Boom! Crackle! Pop!* Noah turned to look at Faith and it wasn't Faith - it was mer-Faith! She had turned into a mermaid! Faith looked over and announced, "Look! Look behind you!" she said. But, as Noah turned around to see, mist filled in the water.

They went in to find another land. It didn't let them in! They could just about see it. They tried but it didn't work. I guess they'd never find out what happened!

Grace Hart (8)

Pheasey Park Farm Primary School, Great Barr

The Quintuplets In The Jungle

Once, quintuplets were born but, randomly, their parents died. Janice, James, John, Jeremy, and Jacob could talk to animals but not all of them liked them. One night, the quintuplets were snoozing on their leaves. All of their animals were sleeping too. A mean monkey was trying to get all of them. An elephant got him away, but he got Janice and took her to his stone hut.

He locked Janice up in a rusty cage. In the morning, the brothers figured out Janice was missing. They were worried sick. All the brothers and animals were searching everywhere they could!

Paige Webb (9)

Pheasey Park Farm Primary School, Great Barr

In The Forest

Kelly and Tom were walking in the forest. They both saw a gold, magic key in the forest. They carried on walking but, all of a sudden, they stopped because they saw an abandoned warehouse. Suddenly, Kelly and Tom heard people scream, "Help me!" really loudly.

They went round the back of the warehouse and turned the key but it didn't work. So they went round the front and it worked. They went in and there were two people and two baddies. Both of them were fighting the baddies. Tom got hurt, he was really furious. They saved the people!

Ruby Walsh (8)
Pheasey Park Farm Primary School, Great Barr

The Tiniest Rabbit In The World

Zoe was in bed, then suddenly, the house shook and shook and shook some more. Then Zoe's body started tingling. She looked down and there was the tiniest rabbit she had ever seen on her nightdress! It was squeaking like it was talking to her.

Then Zoe saw the rabbit hold up a sign that said: *Help us fight crime, use your superpowers.* Zoe pulled a face and said, "Fine." Then the rabbit held up another sign: *Say, powers grow!* From that day until now, Zoe was fighting crime with... THE TINIEST RABBIT IN THE WORLD!

Esme Tallulah Bagnall (8)

Pheasey Park Farm Primary School, Great Barr

Monster Map

It was a gloomy night at the beach. A girl called Lola saw a map. She picked it up and followed where the map was taking her. She got to her destination. She didn't know what was supposed to happen. Then someone grabbed her.
She screamed. It was a monster. He said, "Complete my quest in fifteen minutes."
"Okay," she said. She kicked the wall and out came a sword. She killed the monster. She kicked the wall again and out came a hammer. She smashed the wall and got out. She was so happy. She saw her scared parents.

Kimiya Knight
Pheasey Park Farm Primary School, Great Barr

The Battle With Ursus

Once upon a time, there was a little boy called Jocko. He was the village's hero when anything bad happened. One day, the sky was grey and, trust me, when the sky was grey, it meant something bad was happening. But, when the citizens stepped outside, they were in disbelief. It was the return of the cave troll: Ursus!

As soon as Jocko heard everyone yelling and screaming, he quickly armed up. He went and climbed up the mountains. When he got up, he got a strong arrow and pointed it directly at Ursus. Ursus went straight, directly away.

Alfie Silver (8)
Pheasey Park Farm Primary School, Great Barr

The Phone

Once upon a time, there was a cute girl called Delilah. She loved the forest and her mother finally let her go today! Little did she know, there was a surprise waiting for her. When Delilah arrived at the forest, she found a phone. Being the curious girl she was, she picked it up.
When she got home, she turned the phone on and she found it was unlocked! Delilah found an app and she started taking pictures on it. Soon enough, her face disappeared! Everyone was afraid of her. She tried to find the criminal, but she really couldn't!

Skyla' Jai Nevers-Hamilton (9)
Pheasey Park Farm Primary School, Great Barr

Battle Of Robokon

One day, Trevor was farming potatoes when a soldier charged forward. A battle was happening. He picked up his axe and charged at the enemy. He must have destroyed 1000 of them by the time he stopped and dashed to the robot palace to destroy them all.

Lots of robots attacked him. Wearily, he hit them with the back of the axe and dived into a room. The door closed automatically. He grabbed a book called the Book of Leader Humans and found, weirdly, his dad. It said, *Killed by robots*. So he ran out and destroyed all robots.

Brendan Swain (8)
Pheasey Park Farm Primary School, Great Barr

Save The Horse

Molly had until sunset to save a gracious farm, but could Molly do it? Hopefully before it all burned down. She had to travel through England.
"Woah, this is so fun. No. We've got to focus."
Molly got off the plane. She asked a person, "Do you know where the fire extinguisher is?"
"Yeah, it's in a house."
Molly ran in. "Yes, here it is," said Molly. "Let's go back quick!" Molly had to go all the way back on the plane. The plane went up, then they were there.

Scarlett Owen (8)
Pheasey Park Farm Primary School, Great Barr

Eric Discovering His True Self

Eric sets off on a journey from his mansion to an island and discovers himself for who he is for life. Soon, Eric gets to the island. Then he jumps off his yacht and walks around for a while. Then he finds a monkey and becomes the monkey's friend. Then they set off together quickly, they find a cave in the jungle. Eric and the monkey are pleased. They wander further into the cave until they reach a dead-end. The monkey presses a button, a door opens. They go through, curious what will happen. Eric touches a crystal and changes...

Joshua Goulbourne (9)
Pheasey Park Farm Primary School, Great Barr

City Of The Stars

I have until sunset to find the lost treasure of the stars. It will take many days but I'm sure I'll be able to do it. Right this second, I am flying in my dazzling spaceship to find the cave the treasure is hidden in.

Right now, I'm walking inside the dark gloomy cave. It looks like there is something very shiny in the distance. I'm going to have a look. *Wow!* I think I've found the treasure. This is the best day of my life! I'm going to take this back home to the City of Stars. I'm amazing!

Evie Lester (9)
Pheasey Park Farm Primary School, Great Barr

Magical Keys

In a forest, a little seven-year-old girl named Emily found a magical key. After ten minutes, she found a cottage with the exact same keyhole for the key. Emily ran and put the key into the gap. She ran inside to a table with a purple key.

"What's that?" she said when she found the purple key. Emily woke up Infecteds! The Infecteds stared at Emily. She tried the key but it didn't work. Emily saw a sword for killing that terrible spread. She fought and unexpectedly won. Emily found the truth. She tried the key.

Scarlett Carpenter (8)
Pheasey Park Farm Primary School, Great Barr

The Cursed Diamond

I had until sunset to find out how to destroy the cursed diamond because Earth would be destroyed. I searched my room and found a vent but then I called my friends. They brought a screwdriver, then we opened the vent and hopped into the vent and found the diamond.
Suddenly, a beast appeared and we took our swords and fought. But then another appeared and killed the beasts. Thankfully, the other two partners killed the secret witch, then broke the cursed diamond. I went home and met Mum and Dad and had some coffee and a chat.

Harshiv Tuteja (8)
Pheasey Park Farm Primary School, Great Barr

Jake And The Genie

Once, there was a boy called Jake. He was in the middle of the hot desert. There was a lamp which said: *Make wishes*. Jake made one. Jake waited three seconds. Then he appeared in a room with an evil genie who had powers.

Jake tried to steal the powers. When they had to sleep, he saw the power in the room. He'd dropped his power. Jake took the power, he killed the guards. He was so thrilled to kill the genie and take the power. He took the power, killed the genie and the last guard, and flew off.

Muhammad Ayaan Arshad (9)

Pheasey Park Farm Primary School, Great Barr

Mr Oogie Doogie

I was setting off to find that noise. I'd heard multiple screams. There was some sort of monster eating animals. Finally, I set off to the cave. More screams came. I was very scared, nevertheless, I went in!

It was a maze. There were animals that weren't moving, they were rotting. Bones were on the damp floor. It was sticky. Mr Oogie Doogie was there. He swiped his dirty claws, at my gem that kept me safe. I stabbed him with a sword. After that, he touched my gem and suddenly faded to dust and died.

Michael Dawes (9)
Pheasey Park Farm Primary School, Great Barr

Beast Quest

One day, I heard a deafening roar. There was a T-rex killing a brachiosaurus. We were running to find the T-rex when, suddenly, there was an earthquake. But it was Mount Hector, the volcano. This place was a deserted island. Now there was a hurricane.

We were on the move to find shelter. We found the colossal T-rex, it was there towering over us. There was a tsunami and the weather was getting worse. We needed to find shelter, now! Maybe there was a cave in the mountain, or a tent to put up for shelter.

Ryley Bates (8)
Pheasey Park Farm Primary School, Great Barr

The Sparkly Stone

In a forest, there was a sparkly stone. As Melodie was a curious girl, she picked it up. She picked it up and she went to another universe. She had to be back or she would be in trouble. Melodie was scared because there were aliens. She just wanted to go home.

She still had the stone and she saw humans. She found out that the stone was magical, so she used it. Everyone was saved and they went home. Melodie was still there so she could defeat the aliens and she did. She kept the wonderful, amazing stone.

Ameya Lamichhane (9)
Pheasey Park Farm Primary School, Great Barr

A Curse Of A Voice

One day, there was a boy called Sully. He was not very smart and his friend Tom lost his voice. Sully didn't know what to do. His mum gave him her phone. He found out what to do. He thought he didn't understand. All it said was, the little one screamed at the big one, and he didn't know what sign language was.

His mum kept saying, "Let's just give up."

Sully got really angry, then he started to scream at his mum. Suddenly, a starfish came out and his voice came back!

Mariam Georgiou (8)

Pheasey Park Farm Primary School, Great Barr

Sky Castle

Once, there was a boy named Marly and he had just been in a plane crash and landed on the whitest, largest cloud. Marly didn't want to look behind him but he did. He saw the blackest castle he had ever seen.

"Are you okay?" said a small voice. It was Calum. Calum was the poor scribe of the evil devil. Calum explained what had happened.

"Oh dear," worried Marly. He looked behind his shoulder and a guard shot him and Marly in the eye. They were dead. The castle had gone.

Gracie Doidge (8)
Pheasey Park Farm Primary School, Great Barr

Menacing Maze

Zarah had fallen into a fairytale but she fell into an evil one! She and her brother were doing the first puzzle and earned another diamond. She had to get all four gems to complete her quest. Little did she know, that a creepy spirit was sneaking up on her.

Zarah and her brother Jack were cutting out keys to get out. Suddenly, the monster captured Jack! He was going to be put into a boiling pot of slime! The maze was crumbling apart and she couldn't get to her brother. Was she going to jump?

Ruby Hill (9)

Pheasey Park Farm Primary School, Great Barr

Olivia And The Witch

In the middle of a sea, there was a glimmer. Olivia, who was a girl, swam to discover it. She picked it up and, while she was swimming, she saw a mysterious cave. The item she had was the same size to put it in the hole in the door.

Once she opened the door, she saw a plain piece of paper that said: *You must find a mysterious object to save your friend.* Minutes after she found out and opened the door, she saw a witch and the door ended up closing and locking. That was to trap Olivia.

Imogen Tang
Pheasey Park Farm Primary School, Great Barr

Fire Adventure

We had to get across the rapids to stop the volcano from erupting and destroying the village. We had to get going, three, two, one, jump! Now, to the volcano. We got some materials to block the big eruption from killing everyone. We got some stuff to cover the volcano from erupting. It was nighttime, we had until daytime at 12:00 in the afternoon.

No, the tide was coming in. We had to hurry up and get some more materials. What was that? We had to get back to the house. Okay, back to sleep.

Lewis Wilkins
Pheasey Park Farm Primary School, Great Barr

The Kidnapper

There was a boy in England, then the boy went on a plane to Las Vegas. He had a map because he was going to a water park. Then a man came by in a black van. Then the man came out of the van and the man kidnapped the boy.

The boy woke up in a room but the boy was tied to a chair and he was handcuffed. Then the kidnapper came into the room. Then he said, "What is your name?"

The boy said, "My name is Bob."

Then the man said, "This is an escape room."

Owen Howard (9)
Pheasey Park Farm Primary School, Great Barr

Game Is On

One day, Lucky was doing some computer work when, all of a sudden, she teleported into the computer! She didn't know what to say or do, but what she did know was that she had to complete all two games to get all two stars so the curse would be broken.

The first game was Mario. Lucky had to finish the obstacle course to get her first star. She found it hard but, in the end, she managed to get her first star. The second game was Just Dance. This was easy. Two stars were completed!

Francesca Hall (8)
Pheasey Park Farm Primary School, Great Barr

Survive

I was at the beach on a scorching morning when an ominous robot came stomping up the shore. Suddenly, the robot opened and a witch flew out! As quick as a flash, the witch threw a potion at me and I started to feel myself shrink! A dark shadow loomed above me and the robot was about to stomp on me! I dodged out of the way just in time. After that, a bottle of green liquid smashed on the floor and it soaked into my shoes. I soared up into the sky. I was back to normal size again!

Amy Mather
Pheasey Park Farm Primary School, Great Barr

Devil's Treasure

Once upon a time, Ralf and Winter were walking in the forest when they found an old, creepy house. In the kitchen, Ralf found a gold treasure chest full of money. As the devil came down the stairs, Ralf and Winter hid around the corner. The devil took the chest outside and put it underground.
Ralf fell fast asleep on the floor. Winter woke him up just as the devil started to chase them. As Winter ran outside, she grabbed the treasure chest, and her and Ralf quickly ran home.

Dylan Minshull
Pheasey Park Farm Primary School, Great Barr

Unicorn Quest

I had until sunset to find the Queen Unicorn. She was ill, so I had to save her. So I went to find a daisy and a rose. I found the daisy and rose, then I rode my horse, Sapphire, back to the Magical Meadow. I wasn't sure if it would help heal her. Guess what? It worked! The Queen Unicorn was back on her feet. So I said goodbye to everyone and rode back home on Sapphire. Once I got home, a big surprise was waiting for me. It was that Sapphire was having babies! What?

Felicity Mckeon (8)
Pheasey Park Farm Primary School, Great Barr

Stuck In The Maze

I woke up and found myself stuck in a maze. At first, I was scared but I found a map and built up my courage and started to look around. I found an opening but, before I could walk through, it closed. A few walls started to close around me. I thought I was going crazy.

A bottle of water was standing on a box in front of me. I took a sip and the escape opened. I ran towards it and jumped through. I was relieved to be back in my house. I got into bed and fell asleep.

Lexi Ashford (8)

Pheasey Park Farm Primary School, Great Barr

Shetland Pony Lost In The Snow

One day, I was riding my horse, Ruby, for a hack in the snow. Suddenly, I saw a Shetland pony in the park. So I went into the park to save him. Then I got off Ruby and calmed Tommy boy down. After he was calmed, I galloped back home on Ruby to get the trailer to get Tommy boy home to warm him up. Luckily we had one stable. Then I asked my mum to call horse farms. A while later, we found the owner of Tommy boy. I was happy for Tommy boy. I missed him a lot.

Lilly William (8)
Pheasey Park Farm Primary School, Great Barr

Bob And Max

Once upon a time, there was a boy called Bob and he was on a journey to save someone called Max. He was locked in a cellar, far away, in a cave. Bob had to save Max from the cave. First, Bob had to get to the cave. Then get Max out.

So Bob set off to save Max. Over the hill, then over the mountain and he was there. But he had to get Max out. He tried to find the key and found it. He got Max out and travelled back home to their house safely.

Abby Skelton
Pheasey Park Farm Primary School, Great Barr

Kill A Monster

I opened the box that was glowing and I suddenly fell asleep. When I woke up, the box was glowing some more, so I went to move it but it gave me an electric shock and I was in a cave by myself. My hand was hurting. I went out of the cave and there I saw a big monster standing there. I tried to defeat it so I must've got out when I was asleep. I went to defeat it so I stabbed it one hundred times and it died. Victory dance time!

Ethan Allmark (9)
Pheasey Park Farm Primary School, Great Barr

Treasure In The Jungle

One day, a boy called Rowan was in a jungle. The boy was very brave. He was walking and he saw a bunch of monkeys. They were quite small. He got the key from them. He was walking along and he found a chest. He opened the chest, it needed the key. He found a bunch of treasure. He found crystals, gold, he found all sorts. It was so good.

Harrison Oneill
Pheasey Park Farm Primary School, Great Barr

The Dark Secret Of The Rainforest

The deafening roar echoed in my ears while my whole body trembled with overwhelming fear. My quest for survival in this dense, deadly rainforest had just accelerated. Courageously, I peered between the trees and saw the most extraordinary creature. The size of an enormous dog but with majestic, golden, feathered wings. This was the most bizarre species I'd ever seen. Staring through me, its piercing, fiery eyes made me freeze with terror.

Fearing the end, I suddenly felt a hand grab my shoulder, pulling me hard. At breakneck speed, we disappeared into the darkness. But where were we headed?

Ethan Reddivari (10)
Red House School, Norton

Tick, Tick, Tick

The train roared toward the station. William searched. Where could it be? The signal box, lost luggage, the waiting room? Courageous William looked around. Finally, he saw it - the track. *Tick, tick, tick.* Time raced. The train zoomed closer. William ran like he had never run before. He panted breathlessly. Could he change the points in time? He pulled the lever as the train rushed past. It diverted onto the mountain line.

Phew! He felt exhausted. Could he defuse the bomb? He sprinted to the track. William desperately picked up the bomb and threw it into the river. *Boom!*

William Moore (7)
Red House School, Norton

The Dutchman's Treasure Hunt

Once, there were two friends called George and Jack. They lived in a very silent village near a huge volcano that was still active. One day, George's grandpa gave him a treasure map which was the Dutchman's route! The next day, George and Jack left early and went for an adventure.

The map took them to a broken bridge that was rotten and had partly fallen down. They went carefully through the bridge and finally discovered the Dutchman's treasure. Suddenly, they heard a loud noise that came from the smoking mountain. The volcano erupted splashing ash, rocks and lava everywhere.

Leon Tanttari (8)
Red House School, Norton

The Voyage Of The Hidden Jewel

I had until sunset to find the hidden jewel. My village depended on it. I took a deep breath and continued through the jungle. After four hours, I found a cave. A roar came from deep within. I froze.

"Keep going," I muttered. I kept walking and, suddenly, a creature with flaming, red eyes slithered out of the darkness.

"You shall not enter," it thundered.

Without thinking, I stabbed the beast with my sword and ran into the blackness. There it was, the grand chest. I opened it and... there was nothing! The hidden jewel was still out there somewhere.

Genevieve Reily (10)
Red House School, Norton

An Unbroken Curse

Treacherously navigating the side of the cliff, I eventually came to the elusive entrance of the dark, damp, heavily concealed cave. I found hidden strength to move the ominous boulder.

The stench of dampness almost overcame me. The ancient stones were covered in mould. I was drawn to one in particular. I could almost make out a medieval image of torture. This image had inflicted so much pain on so many. I viciously scraped the image with my pocket knife while feeling the agony release from my body. That stone became a blank canvas for the world to heal itself.

Hugo Duncan-Whitfield (11)

Red House School, Norton

The Rescue Mission Of Amelia Chante

The plan was set. Three, two, one, go! As I shapeshifted into a tiny caterpillar to get through the drain, Lia, the Princess of Fire and Water, got the washing line, that was on fire, ready. I scaled the wall with ease and gave the signal. Teardrop. Lia dropped the line which melted the wax drains, allowing my friends to jump through the holes. The boys, Leo, Tommy, and Daniel, fought Marco and his bodyguards while me and Betty, the Princess of Technology, picked the cage and released my sister, Amelia, from her imprisonment. Then I shouted, "Get out now!"

Naina Kurup (10)
Red House School, Norton

The Christmas Monster

Every Christmas it's the same - there's always some mysterious thing that happens! Lights are lit around the street, Christmas decorations are everywhere. People all come out to celebrate the miracle, but Mr Brown hates it all and takes all his lights and decorations off. But they kept appearing and he had to leave them on. One day, the strangest thing happened. Mr Brown started to enjoy Christmas! I went to bed and woke up and saw the Christmas monster decorating. Suddenly, she turned around and winked at me! I ran downstairs and at my door was a present.

Maia Olbrich (10)
Red House School, Norton

The Factory-Made Monster

I found the switch. I couldn't believe it, it was under my nose the entire time. I flipped it. I tumbled down a seemingly infinite drop. I landed in a gigantic room. Suddenly, the machinery started making noises, scaring me.

Out from a blocky machine came a monster made out of goo! It proceeded to cover anything it touched in the sticky concoction, including me! I awoke in a cage hanging above acid. The monster was standing by me.

I pulled out my heated knife. I melted the bars to escape from that horrible cage. I locked that switch forever.

Eddison Williams (10)

Red House School, Norton

A Voyage Beneath

The ship juddered to a halt. We had arrived! Aiden said, "Are you ready to go diving for the lost treasure?"

I replied, "Ready as I'll ever be." And we put on our suits and completed the final checks. "Ready!"

We stood on the back of the ship. "Three, two, one, go!" We jumped off. Wow! Immediately, there was an array of colours. The fish looked stunning but we knew that we had to go further. And we did. We kept going until finally, we found it! We hoisted the treasure up and began our climb to the top.

Adam Khaliq (10)
Red House School, Norton

Calamitous Time In Anfield

One evening, I stepped into a mysterious portal. I realised I was at Anfield Stadium. All I could remember was that I was there to help the players find their boots. So I started searching everywhere, in the toilets, pitch, and locker room. I thought I'd searched everywhere until I realised I hadn't searched the trophy room. It was so high up.
A few minutes after, I met Trent and we agreed to search together. When we reached the top, I saw them. I couldn't believe I'd met Trent and I'd also found the boots. What an amazing day!

Harry Oo (10)
Red House School, Norton

The Monster

She took a deep breath and took out her sword. The creature was a gloomy, muddy-type colour, it also had three rather large eyes which made you feel possessed if you looked directly at them. A ginormous, seven-foot body towered over her, brown warts covered the majority of its body. She lunged toward it.

The beast was nothing like she'd expected. It wasn't startled by her. In fact, he charged at her, attempting to scratch her eyes out. Once he turned his back, she took her chance and stabbed him in the back. She watched him bleed to death.

Isobel Haywood (10)
Red House School, Norton

Earth's Saviour

I had until sunset to slay the ghastly beast. It had already devoured my whole family. It grew stronger by the night, it was already strong enough to single-handedly obliterate a small country. If it grew any stronger, planet Earth would be doomed.

I started my journey up Mount Fuji. The beast's footprints led me to the peak. Hours later, I found a mysterious cave entrance. An ear-piercing roar came from the beast. It charged at me. I flung my father's hatchet at him. It went clean through the monster's neck. The world was saved.

Finley Williamson (11)
Red House School, Norton

The Search For Gaara

We had until daybreak but it was too late, Gaara had been consumed by the five-tailed beast. I trembled with terror and the sun rose as they disappeared into the distance - but I couldn't stop there!

I finally built up enough courage to stop Gaara, *but how?* I thought. The only solution was to assemble the nine-tailed fox, a beast so magnificently strong, its power can't be comprehended. Although this task couldn't be succeeded by one man, I had to find allies. I set off to find my squad - my fate was yet to be decided.

Luke Gardner (11)
Red House School, Norton

The Clock

I stepped up into an old, damp-smelling room. From the corner of my eye, I spotted a tall grandfather clock with a mirrored door. There was a note that read, in bold letters: *Don't change the time.* When I saw it, I couldn't resist reaching out. I turned the small hand to eight.

My reflection caught my eye - I was older. I was curious now. I had to turn it again. Ten o'clock. Now my hair was grey. I wondered what would happen at midnight. My shaking hand reached for the clock and moved the hand. Twelve... I was gone.

Iris McGlynn (10)
Red House School, Norton

The Mysterious Bottles

I opened the glowing box. Suddenly, there was a bang! I turned around to see two bottles of glowing liquid. I didn't think anything at first. Then, to my surprise, the box stopped glowing and then the bottles stopped. I didn't know what to do. I looked around and looked, but nothing was there. I picked the bottles up and shook them up until my arms nearly dropped off. When I thought there was no hope, the biggest glow I had ever seen shone straight through me. It sent an icy blast through me. I was petrified! Everything fell silent.

Erin Hodgson (10)
Red House School, Norton

The Mischief Begins

It was the first of December, I woke to the sound of mumbling. I lifted my head, peeking over my duvet. In the moonlight, I caught the stare of one of my Christmas elves.

With smirks on their faces, they threw magic dust into the air. Suddenly, I felt tingling as I began to shrink to the size of my elves. They grabbed my paint and hurried out of the room. I quickly followed into my parents' bedroom. With the flick of a brush, they had glasses and moustaches on their faces. I couldn't wait to see what happened tomorrow!

Isabella Riley (10)
Red House School, Norton

A Magic Man

Once upon a time, there was a magical wizard called Pelsh. He could cast a spell that could explode the moon. But, one day, there was a man who came and stole his magical staff. Then the fun began.

He had to travel across the big, blue ocean and the gigantic Grand Canyon until he reached the cave of the wizard gods. He chanted a spell and then *screech!* The doors dragged themselves to the side. Pelsh waddled into the dark cave, where he saw a big beam of light shining down on him. Then, all of a sudden, *bang!*

Kayden Duffey (10)
Red House School, Norton

The Wish Deer

Mother coughed constantly in the woven rocking chair beside the fire. The image of her suffering was vivid in my mind. Fog rolled towards the edge of the Shadowed Forest, gripping my feet and pulling me into darkness. I was there to seek medicine for my ill and sick mother.

I felt blind until a small blur of light illuminated my surroundings. The Wish Deer. One look into his eyes would grant you only one wish. I glared at him, wishing for a treatment for my mother. I felt hot and knew he had seen me and granted my wish.

Faith Hall (11)
Red House School, Norton

Imagination

As I scrambled to get my ball out of the bush, I heard a squeak at the back. It was a gate opening. I nervously walked to the gate, my legs just stopped, and then I was on a massive football pitch playing against professional footballers. I felt diminutive to everyone. I felt stupendous.
I was playing for Tottenham Hotspur. Harry Kane passed me the ball over the top of the other team and I went and scored in the top corner. The atmosphere was unreal. Then, all of a sudden, I was just playing football outside my house.

Jenson Harte (10)
Red House School, Norton

The Tongue-Twister

Today, the most out of the ordinary thing happened to me. My teacher, Miss Half, was showing us maps and her hands started to grow. Her spine shot up so she was like a giraffe. Her skin turned pink and green, with spikes running down her back. She then picked up my friend, but not with her hands, with her bright orange tongue. She started to swing my friend around like she was on a ride at a theme park. She then stopped and dropped her onto the floor, *bang!* All I heard my friend say was, "... wake up!"

Brontë Marin (10)
Red House School, Norton

The Lost Friend

I'd found the key but not the cave. I didn't know what to do but then I saw the map.

The cave was nearby, as the map told me, but what I didn't realise was, it was behind the wall next to me.

The wallpaper fell and revealed a huge stone wall with a keyhole engraved into the rock.

I had found my friend, but there were things stopping me, like dart shooters.

I was almost at the end, I felt it.

Then I saw him!

We had to get out quick, as the cave was collapsing in on itself!

Dylan Hodgson Wood (10)
Red House School, Norton

The Trapped Fox

On a frosty, cold morning, Lola woke up to her sister being gone. She checked the windows and saw footprints, so she packed her bag and left. Lola followed the prints as she started hearing whimpering yelps from the forest.

She walked further in the gloomy forest to find her sister next to a fox in a trap. She got her pliers and cut the trap, then gave the fox warm milk and let it go. Lola and her sister then went home to their parents and told them how they'd saved a fox from a trap in the forest.

Robynne Mclaren (11)
Red House School, Norton

The Boy Who Woke Up To Be A Footballer

Once upon a time, there was a boy called Max. He loved playing football. One day, he had his dinner and went to bed and when he woke up he was an adult! He got dressed and rushed out, there was a Ferrari! He switched on the news and it said Max had scored the winning goal in the Euro 2040. He felt ecstatic. He wanted to go to his family but he didn't know where they were.

The phone rang. He picked it up. A voice said, "We need you for the football World Cup in Spain, Max Peterson."

Samira Arun (8)
Red House School, Norton

The Five Broken Parts (Part One)

Once upon a time, there was a boy. His name was Chris and he was always excited for Christmas. He thought it was the best event of the year! But in his dreams, there was a deep, dark tale to be told. So this was a nightmare. He was in a dead campsite, there was a blood-curdling scream, but there was a deep voice saying, "If you find all five parts of a cuddly bear, now you should set off and find them, if you do, you win. If you lose you will stay here forever, hahaha. You will suffer."

Ashton Chapman (9)
Red House School, Norton

Arya The Saviour

I raced to the empty cell... she'd been moved! I had
to find Esperanza. I wrote down a report of my
missing friend under my name, Arya Goldenheart. I
had finally found that her location was in Paris.
By the next night, I'd found her lying in a cell, no
food or water. She told me where the master keys
were, so I sneaked and got them. When I got back,
we both tried to creep away and nearly got
caught. When we finally got to the hotel I was
staying at, she said Jinx had captured her.

Philippa Vaux (10)
Red House School, Norton

The Mysterious Key

This morning, I woke up and saw an old and rusty key. It also had a very detailed map with the landmarks of the world! Suddenly, a huge, loud rumble startled me. The rusty, old, and manky key fell on the floor.

I ran as fast as I could and kept on running, and then I was at Stone Henge. But something was very odd. There were no other people there. Only one cruel and vicious soul, the Potato Egg, was ready to pounce out at me. But he had already got me. Suddenly, I was back home.

Tobias MacDonald (10)
Red House School, Norton

Broken Heart

When I arrived at the spooky island, Cavetoppia, a horrendous sight greeted me! It was a massive, dark blue, ferocious monster with a glowing heart the size of a football. With his mouth dripping bright red blood! He had claws the size of a lion's and I saw, behind him, a treasure chest.
So I fought the ferocious beast and I found a sword. I stabbed him right in the head. After that, I cut it open, only to find a key to open the chest. The treasure was mine, all mine.

William Robinson (9)
Red House School, Norton

The Mystery Of The Golden Egg

Agent Hartley was nervous as the plane landed in Dubai. Agent Jordan, eating like a carnivore, was not fazed at having only twenty-four hours to find the golden egg! The tracking device showed the dolphin park, the sensor was beeping profusely. They started to run fast. It went off the land and into the water. It was on a jet-ski with the infamous Booth. Both agents jumped on a jet-ski and flew off into the sea, shooting at Booth and putting a hole in his jet-ski.

Harry Bobby Winspear (10)
Red House School, Norton

Surprise Present

Once upon a time, there lived a young girl named Jessica Howlett and this is where her story starts. A long time ago, in a place that you know as the north pole, it was a beautiful day just like any other, but something strange happened. She opened a present that'd come to the door addressed to her. She was excited. Excited because she had never seen anything like it. All of a sudden, the present turned into a wormhole and sucked her in.

Jessica Howlett (9)
Red House School, Norton

Who Did It?

"You know you can trust us. You know, just tell us who killed him."

"Well," said Clover, "it all started when me and Sam were walking down the corridor. We heard our headteacher talking to a bizarre man."

"Just give me some time. I'm sure the person will turn themselves in soon," explained the headteacher.

"What the heck?" said Sam.

"That's exactly what I was going to say." We went to the hall, not knowing the words of our headteacher would change our lives forever.

"Everyone, I'm here to say: Ian was killed yesterday. Now, who did it?"

Kashaya Yakou (11)
St John's Primary School, Liverpool

Finding The Truth

"Sam? Hello? Oh, you're awake," Sally said.

"What?" I said because I'd just woken up.

"Oh, nothing," she said.

"Okay," I said.

I looked at my mother and father's photo because they'd died when I was a child. I wondered about my family for a few minutes, saying I wanted to find out my family's life and truth.

I booked two tickets to the jungle because that was the first place. Me and Sally got to the jungle and met a girl who knew about my family. Her name was Zoe, she told me to go with her...

Dana Conroy (10)

St John's Primary School, Liverpool

The Bizarre Mountain

Once, there was a boy with the name Jonathan. He loved exploring mountains. However, one day, he started exploring a very bizarre mountain. He could feel sweat running down his face. He put himself together and went on.

Jonathan heard screams. He went to explore the noise, when he saw a woman tied up. Thankfully, he had the strength to free her. However, they met a guy with fire in his eyes. Annabelle, the woman, and Jonathan were trembling. Although they thought they would die, the man helped them escape. Then another creature killed them. They were never seen again.

Maya Cyron (10)
St John's Primary School, Liverpool

Bob And The Cursed Necklace

Bob awoke with a start, ready for his journey. Running into the cursed and abandoned castle, he looked through the dining room, seeing golden enemies with horns, like on a bull's head. He dashed through the next room until he saw a glowing object. It burned his eyes. He saw it was a golden necklace. It suddenly flew up, summoning skeletal soldiers with glowing purple eyes. He looked around for a weapon to defend himself and saw a spear with a stone inside it. He destroyed the soldiers. The necklace dropped. He stabbed the cursed, sinister item, destroying it forever.

Patrick O'Sullivan (11)
St John's Primary School, Liverpool

Alex And The Chasing Of The Golden Chalice

Alex was awakened by the smell of a new adventure. He quickly packed his things for the adventure and he started up his ATV. His new quest was to locate the golden chalice in the jungle and secretly steal the chalice from the temple of the jungle gods. Alex started his journey but had to pass some booby traps and obstacles to complete his quest. He was trying to get hold of the mysterious golden chalice because it was worth 629 million pounds. Alex's dream was to become an adventurous person who lived a wealthy life. Alex dodged flying arrows.

Antoni Warcholik (10)
St John's Primary School, Liverpool

The Mysterious Box

I was eager to open the ancient and forbidden box laying there before my eyes. My lips parted slightly with curiosity at what was inside. I was desperate to open it but my gut instinct told me not to. A few moments passed just looking at it, so I decided to open it. When I did, something wasn't right. The atmosphere was eerie. Suddenly, out of the blue, a gust of wind hit my face and lightning struck. My surroundings changed and lightning struck. My surroundings changed, I was in the middle of nowhere with trees twisting and towering above.

Laurie Faragher (10)
St John's Primary School, Liverpool

The Demon Soul

One day there was a priest visiting the woods for a stroll. All of a sudden, he stumbled upon a haunted house. Father Michael had read about it in a news article, where there was a house in the middle of the woods that was haunted by a poltergeist roaming around the house in a little boy's body. As Father Michael was approaching the house, the front door swung wide open. Father Michael went into the house and a sudden cold sweat ran down his face. The next day, Father Michael was reported missing. The mystery was never solved.

Lola Jarman (11)
St John's Primary School, Liverpool

Aqua And Flame War

One day, there lived a boy called Inferno. He was the fire demon's son. He was loved by everyone in Volcanic City. There was someone who was jealous of him and wanted to take him out, his name was Aqua. Everyone feared him, so he moved out and made his own kingdom in the ocean.

One day, Aqua decided to attack Volcanic City and kill Inferno once and for all, and become King of Volcanic City. So he invaded Volcanic City and lost to Inferno and never tried to invade again. Inferno was even more famous from then on.

Jacob Draper (11)
St John's Primary School, Liverpool

The Abandoned Island

I woke up with a headache in the middle of nowhere, but on an island. I was trekking through the jungle while hearing and watching all of the beautiful animals and flowers: sunflowers, roses, and beautiful deer. I took my eyes off them and continued my journey to find the truth. As I continued my journey, it started getting dark and I wanted to rest my eyes for a minute. But I kept going on my journey and then I saw a way out. There was an unusual door, it was glowing. I jumped in and I was at home.

Hawi Haydar (10)
St John's Primary School, Liverpool

Space Train

John, a ten-year-old boy from Newcastle, got very lucky one Christmas day. This is how it happened. The day before Christmas, he was asleep until he heard a knock on his window. He went to check. His eyes lit up as he saw a flying train hovering above the house.

The train conductor said, "Come on, get on, John." Still thinking it was a dream, John got on. There were only four people on the train. First was a pair of twins, Joey and Harry, they already knew each other.

John Shaw (10)
St John's Primary School, Liverpool

The Treasure Hunt

I've found the secret map to find the treasure chest. Sammy wants to know what is in it, maybe money, or a key for the other chest. Sammy has no idea where it is. He really wants to know where it is. Oh, I should look at my map so then I know where it is. What! It's in the ocean! Why am I on land? I need to get on a boat to get to the ocean. A few days later, Sammy is finally there and we are confused. But then we look at the ocean and it's there.

Tomas Lee (10)
St John's Primary School, Liverpool

Tomas The Kid Spy

Tomas was a spy about to go on a mission to a mysterious island. He was in a weird location on the island. He went to look for help like he wasn't a spy. He went to look for food and shelter for the night. He was on this mission to break a curse. He went hunting for food. One hour later, he found a wild pig. The problem was, he never had a spear or a knife, so he tried to find a rock by him. He went to find a rock in the bushes.

Sammy Draper (10)
St John's Primary School, Liverpool

YOUNG WRITERS
INFORMATION

We hope you have enjoyed reading this book – and that you will continue to in the coming years.

If you're a young writer who enjoys reading and creative writing, or the parent of an enthusiastic poet or story writer, do visit our website **www.youngwriters.co.uk**. Here you will find free competitions, workshops and games, as well as recommended reads, a poetry glossary and our blog. There's lots to keep budding writers motivated to write!

If you would like to order further copies of this book, or any of our other titles, then please give us a call or order via your online account.

Young Writers
Remus House
Coltsfoot Drive
Peterborough
PE2 9BF
(01733) 890066
info@youngwriters.co.uk

Join in the conversation!
Tips, news, giveaways and much more!

 **YoungWritersUK** 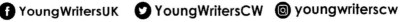 **YoungWritersCW**  **youngwriterscw**